To order additional copies of this book, contact
Toll Free +65 3165 7531 (Singapore)
Toll Free +60 3 3099 4412 (Malaysia)
www.partridgepublishing.com/singapore
orders.singapore@partridgepublishing.com

ISBN
ISBN: 978-1-5437-6828-2 (sc)
ISBN: 978-1-5437-6830-5 (hc)
ISBN: 978-1-5437-6829-9 (e)

Print information available on the last page.

02/04/2022

PARTRIDGE

DARK

Preston PL

I would like to thank my wife, Ha, and our sons Kym & John for their continued support and listening to my stories, hoping that one day I would turn my words into pages.

My name is Lukewarm, and I would like to share the true story of my fear of the dark.

Dusk Primary School

As soon as I heard my mum's voice, I knew daylight had finally arrived and would jump out of bed, have a quick clean-up, eat breakfast, and be on my way to school. 'Do not forget your lunch,' Mum would say!

I really enjoyed school, learning, having fun with my friends, and getting up to mischief—sometimes!

Boiling-Hot, Radar, and Blister are my best friends. We would play sky-racing. I never won, but we had such great fun together.

On the way home from school, we would walk and talk about all the fun we had throughout the day and would wave goodbye until tomorrow.

When I got home, I would drop my school bag at the door and run straight to the kitchen cupboard for something to eat. 'Wait for your dinner, please,' Mum would say!

Glaring at me, Mum would ask, 'Do you have homework?' I would shrug my shoulders and quickly get ready for dinner.

After dinner, I would help Mum clean up, then we would watch television around a warm fire.

'Off to bed now. It is late, and you have school tomorrow,' Mum would say. I would hug Mum and slowly make my way to bed.

I dreaded going to bed. I was so scared of the dark. Dad would tuck me in, turn off the light, and close the door. I could feel the dark creep into my room and over my bed.

I could see shadowy figures moving towards me. They would not go away even when I closed my eyes.

Coldness would come upon me; I would pull the blanket over my eyes, daring not to look over it.

The blanket felt heavy. I was terrified that someone was on my bed.

I lay motionless, afraid to move or make a sound, each breath silent and shallow.

I moved down under the blanket until I reached the bottom of the bed. I lay there holding the blanket tight around me, peering towards my pillow, wishing night-time would turn into daytime, gradually falling into a deep sleep.

Suddenly I heard, 'Awake. You will be late for school.' I was so happy. As soon as I heard Mum's voice, I knew the light of day had finally arrived.

I am a little older now, and my fear of the dark comes and goes. A calm moonlit sky brings a good night's sleep, until dark creeps in once more.